RUN
for the
MONEY

Books by Scott Corbett

RUN
for the
MONEY

by SCOTT CORBETT

Illustrated by Bert Dodson

An Atlantic Monthly Press Book
Little, Brown and Company
BOSTON   TORONTO

COPYRIGHT © 1973 BY SCOTT CORBETT

FIRST EDITION

T 10/73

Library of Congress Cataloging in Publication Data

Corbett, Scott.
  Run for the money.

    SUMMARY: Asked to deliver a mysterious package an
unlikely sleuth discovers he has almost abetted a ring
of thieves.
    "An Atlantic Monthly Press book."
    [1. Mystery stories] I. Dodson, Bert, illus.
II. Title.
PZ7.C79938Ru   [Fic]   73-5971
ISBN 0-316-15707-4

ATLANTIC—LITTLE, BROWN BOOKS
ARE PUBLISHED BY
LITTLE, BROWN AND COMPANY
IN ASSOCIATION WITH
THE ATLANTIC MONTHLY PRESS

*Published simultaneously in Canada
by Little, Brown & Company (Canada) Limited*
PRINTED IN THE UNITED STATES OF AMERICA

To

HOWARD STERN

coin collector,

with thanks for some

timely assistance

RUN
for the
MONEY

1

THE first thing Steve heard that summer morning was a news item on the radio about a big robbery. Burglars had broken into the house of a local millionaire and stolen a lot of furs and jewelry.

Steve frowned.

Immediately he was Sherlock O'Neill, scourge of the underworld. He burst into a marble hall, catching no less than five men in the act of removing ten fur coats and a million dollars in diamonds. While he was at it he shot a couple of the men, just to teach them a lesson.

Imagination is a wonderful time-saver. All this bursting in and catching and shooting took place in a matter of seconds. This was just as well. Otherwise, Steve would not have had time for it.

Steve O'Neill had the intent, earnest expression of a boy who did not mean to let a single minute of his stay on this earth slip by without being put to some use. He had so many things he wanted to do they had to stand in line waiting till he could get to them.

The instant he woke up in the morning he would reach over to his bedside table for the big glasses he had to wear. Sitting up in bed, he would give them a rubdown with one of the lens papers he kept with him at all times, on

his bedside table, on his desk, in his pockets. Once they were polished to his satisfaction, he would settle them on the bridge of his curved, owl-like beak.

By then his mind would already have a good start on his plans for the day.

He could never bear to have his glasses anything but spotless and gleaming. This was not because he was fussy about dirt. It was merely part of his burning desire to see everything as clearly and as well as possible. Furthermore, whenever he became excited about anything his face grew red and hot, and that made his glasses mist over.

Needless to say, the large dark-rimmed glasses under his dark eyebrows and over his owl nose made him look that much more earnest and intent. At times when his brown eyes were flashing about something he looked downright fierce.

When he got out of bed that morning, his eyes were flashing.

To see him at the breakfast table a short time later, however, with his head bowed and his hands in his lap, anyone might have thought he was spending a moment in prayer. Anyone but his family, that is. Steve twitched guiltily as his mother appeared from the kitchen. He knew what was coming.

"Stephen O'Neill, how many times have I told you not to bring your coin books to the table?"

His father, who was fond of statistics, replied for him. "Now, let's see. As a conservative estimate, I'd say about two hundred and twenty times."

Caught with the goods, Steve brought his *Guide Book of United States Coins* up from his lap.

"Well, gee," he muttered, "I just wanted to make sure about that 1899 Indian Head . . ."

And even then, as he slowly closed the book on the table beside him, his head was tipping sideways, his eyes prying into the pages for one last lingering look.

"I'll take that," said his mother firmly, and transferred the book to the sideboard. "I suppose you're still trying to make up your mind about your birthday present."

Steve sighed heavily.

"Well, it isn't easy. I think I've decided, but I want to take one more look at what Mr. Jonas has to offer and make sure he isn't trying to stick me with something a grade or two below what it ought to be."

Seven terms were used by collectors to grade the condition of coins. The top grade was *proof,* which referred to coins with a mirrorlike surface that had been struck especially for collectors. Next best was *uncirculated,* meaning coins that had never been used, and therefore remained in mint condition. After those grades came *extremely fine, very fine, fine, very good, good,* and *fair.* Grades in the middle range were often a matter of opinion and a source of argument.

Concerning Steve's birthday present, Amy had an opinion to offer, as older sisters often do.

"If you ask me, I don't think anybody ought to pick out his own birthday present," she declared with an intolerant toss of her teen-age head. "How can a birthday present be a surprise if you pick it out yourself?"

"I don't want any surprises," said Steve. "I know what I want."

"Steve always knows what he wants," said his mother.

"Ha," said Steve.

"And what, may I ask, is the meaning of that 'ha'?"

His owlish face relaxed as he grinned.

"Well, what I want right now and what I'm really after are two different things." His deep-set eyes glazed like marbles behind his big glasses as he schemed into the future. "Sooner or later I'm going to get enough trade bait together, and then I'm going to trade Mr. Jonas out of what I want most of all."

"What's that?" asked Amy.

Steve's face lit up. "A Fugio Cent," he said in a tone of voice only another coin collector would have understood. A flourish of trumpets accompanying the announcement would not have been out of place.

Amy, however, was no coin collector. At that point in their lives about the only interest they had in common was the dinner table, and they did not even like the same things there.

"Fugio!" she said scornfully. "Where's that? I thought you only collected U.S. coins."

Steve groaned at such ignorance.

"Fugio's not a place, dummy, it's a word on the coin. It's Latin, and it means 'time flies.' Fugio Cents were the first coins issued by the United States."

"We started small," suggested Mr. O'Neill.

"That's right," said Steve, smiling loyally at his father's joke. "We started with a penny and worked up to a hundred-thousand-dollar bill with President Woodrow Wilson's picture on it."

"A hundred-thousand-dollar bill! That's not something you're likely to get in your change at a cigar counter."

"Nobody gets them. They're only used for government transactions. The Federal Reserve System and the Treasury Department hand them back and forth."

7

Amy stared at him and took refuge in another attack of teen-age scorn.

"You know the craziest things!"

"Well, it's interesting," claimed Steve. "But the Fugio Cent, now — it's got a sundial in the middle of its obverse side, with 'Fugio' and '1787' beside it, and at the bottom it says 'Mind Your Business.' "

He paused, then added the painful part of the coin's description.

"And Mr. Jonas wants thirty dollars for the one he has."

Mr. O'Neill whistled.

"Thirty smackers! You'll really have to mind your business if you're ever going to own that one."

"I know," said Steve, who had been allotted ten dollars to spend on his birthday present, "but someday . . ."

Amy was appalled at the mere thought of wasting that much money on anything so foolish.

"Thirty dollars! Why, for that kind of money I could buy every record the Lowest Common Denominators ever made!" she said, mentioning her favorite group.

Steve gave them a one-word review.

"Yuk!"

"Oh, you don't know anything about music!"

"Neither do they."

"Now, never mind that, you two," said Mr. O'Neill. "Steve, if you want to ride downtown with me and go see Mr. Jonas, you'd better eat your breakfast."

Steve ate, but his thoughts remained with the Fugio Cent.

2

BEFORE Steve was through, his father had finished and was taking a look at the morning paper.

"Well, I see Ernie Craddock claims those burglars got away with over forty thousand dollars' worth of furs and jewelry last night," he remarked. "By George, nobody's safe any more!"

Since Ernie Craddock happened to be an obnoxious moneygrabber whom most right-thinking people in town could not stand, the other O'Neills failed to greet this news with much indignation, but not Steve. It was not that he cared about the Craddocks. He knew very little about them. It was just that he detested thieves.

"Well, whoever did it, I hope they catch 'em," he burst out, and his face darkened until he looked as cruel as one of those emperors on an old Roman coin. "If I had my way, I'd brand them right on the forehead. I'd cut off their hands, and maybe their noses —"

"Please, Steve, we're eating breakfast!" said his mother, and Amy said, "Just because someone took your silly kite —"

"It's not only my kite! How about the Belmont Collection!" cried Steve, and kept right on looking like the emperor Nero or Caligula. One thing was certain, he had the right nose for it, a real Roman nose.

Amy knew as well as the rest of them that Steve had good reason to hate thieves.

First there had been the trip to New York City he had anticipated with so much excitement because it coincided with the exhibition of a famous coin collection. He had written ahead for the catalogue, and had all but memorized it. He had hardly slept a wink the night before they left for New York.

And that same night, before the exhibition could even open, thieves broke in and stole most of the collection. The exhibition was, of course, canceled. What would have been the highlight of their trip for Steve was turned into a bitter disappointment.

A week later, thieves struck again, and this time closer to home.

Coin collecting was Steve's indoor hobby. Outdoors it was kite flying. He went at both hobbies with the same intensity and drive. For him, kite flying was not mere kid stuff. Kite flying was a sport, an art, and a science, the science of aerodynamics. He belonged to a local club of enthusiasts that included a high school physics teacher, two college professors, and several doctors, lawyers, and bankers, not to mention a retired mailman who was their club champion.

A week after their trip to New York, a brand-new triangular box kite he had built himself disappeared from the tail gate of their station wagon one Sunday out in Sprague Park. He had left it there for only a couple of minutes, but when he returned it was gone.

So Steve had good reason to hate thieves.

When it was time to leave with his father, he rushed to his room to pick up his new kite case. In his hurry he managed to give his right elbow a nasty crack on a doorknob. He hardly paused to rub it, however, because such things were an old story with him.

Steve was not so much awkward as absentminded about where he was going. He was the kind who walked into a lamppost now and then while thinking about something else. Yet when he did anything that demanded and got all his attention and concentration, like flying a kite, he could move with grace and precision.

He was proud of his new kite case, which he had constructed out of a three-foot length of six-inch aluminum tubing scrounged from a friend of the family. An old suitcase handle fastened to it with leather straps made it easy to carry.

In it was a collapsible triangular box kite he had also designed and built to replace the stolen one. With the kite were a reel of No. 15 mason's twine and such other essentials as stripping tape, thread, extra splints, and a small bottle of white glue.

"Where are you going with that thing?" his father asked with understandable concern when Steve came running out to the car. Steve carrying anything large became a Dangerous Moving Object, because he was liable to forget he was carrying it and bump into something or somebody. Either that or leave it somewhere.

"I want it with me, Dad." As usual, he had a full and busy day outlined for himself, taking advantage of every opportunity. "I have to ride the bus home anyway, so I'm going on to Sprague Park and try out my new kite."

"Oh. Well, I guess you're not likely to forget *that* and leave it somewhere. Just don't poke anybody in the back with it getting on the bus."

"I won't."

Steve climbed in the front seat with exaggerated care and set the case upright on the floor between his knees.

"I must say, that outfit is pretty impressive," his father remarked as they drove off.

"If it turns out as well as I hope, and I can get some more tubing from Mr. Kenyon, maybe I'll build some more and sell them."

Mr. O'Neill chuckled.

"Got your eye on that Fugio Cent, haven't you?"

"Well, every little bit will help."

"If you end up owning coins like that, you'll need a safe to keep them in."

"I sure will." The Roman-emperor look darkened Steve's face again, and his glasses seemed to flash fire. "If anyone ever stole *my* collection, I'd — I'd — Well, I don't know what I'd do, but it would be pretty terrible!"

"Brands on foreheads . . . hands chopped off . . . noses missing . . ."

"Worse!"

"Okay, but get that look off your face, you're scaring the other motorists."

The scowl dissolved into a silly grin, and they both laughed. Mr. O'Neill slowed at the corner, swung into traffic, and brought up a new subject. He glanced at his son with a slightly troubled frown.

"You know, I do wish you had someone better to do business with than old Jonas. He annoys me. He's got a heart of gold, that man — the size of a one-dollar gold piece."

"Eighteen forty-nine," said Steve automatically, that being the first year U.S. gold dollars were struck. "Yes, I know, Dad, he's not exactly a philanthropuss —"

"Philanthro*pist*," corrected Mr. O'Neill, "though I don't know but what I like your word better. No, he's no philanthropuss. More of a sourpuss."

"Yes, but the trouble is, he's still the only important stamp and coin dealer in town. And at least he's been pretty nice to me. He's only tried to gyp me a couple of times, and that was before he found out I really knew something about coins."

"A fine reason!"

"Well, anyway, sometimes when he's not too busy he shows me his new stuff, and he's got a great selection."

"Including that Fugio Cent."

"Right!"

When they reached the downtown section, Mr. O'Neill turned into Main Street and let Steve out in front of the Waverly Building.

"Well, good luck. Actually, I suppose it's good for you to have some dealings with an old horse trader like Jonas. You'll learn how to take care of yourself."

Steve laughed through the pain — he had cracked himself a good one on the shin with his kite case as he got out.

"I'll do my best!" he promised.

3

THE Jonas Stamp and Coin Company was on the fifth floor of the Waverly Building. Behind the counter in the small office was a desk, several cabinets, and a safe.

The only furnishings on the customers' side were a shabby leather-covered sofa with a low table in front of it. Mr. Jonas was not the kind of dealer who needed a handsomely decorated ground-floor shop. He was not interested in casual street trade. Serious collectors came looking for him. Besides, much of his business was conducted by mail.

It was a few minutes before nine when Steve took the elevator to the fifth floor. Judging from the silence and dark doors that greeted him when he walked down the long, gloomy corridor, most of the offices were not yet open. Steve remembered his father's comments and grinned as the faded, dingy lettering on the opaque glass panel came into view. Scrooge would have had just such a shop, had he been a stamp and coin dealer. And Scrooge would always have been there early.

Steve tried the knob. Sure enough the door opened.

It opened, and so did Steve's mouth. Instead of being behind the counter as usual, Mr. Jonas was lying like a crumpled scarecrow on the sofa, his face a pasty gray. If his eyes had not been open and moving, Steve would have feared the worst.

14

"Mr. Jonas!"

The gaunt old man's expression lost some of its misery when he saw Steve. He lifted his head feebly for a better look.

"By Jo!"

"What's the matter, Mr. Jonas?"

"It's my ulcer kicking up again. Excitement was too much for me, I guess —"

"What excitement?"

Had he been robbed? Steve glanced wildly around the office for signs of pillage, but saw none. The door of the safe was not open. The display under the glass counter top appeared untouched.

"Steve, you're heaven sent!" said Mr. Jonas, rolling his eyes up piously. Like so many misers, he was a very pious man. He lay back, seemed to gather his thoughts and his strength, and went on. "I just got back from out of town a few minutes ago — took an early bus — and I brought back a valuable set of stamps for an important client. But now I've had to call the rescue squad to come take me to the hospital, and I'm in a jam."

Without even being aware of it, Steve had stood his kite case on end beside him and was digging in his pocket for a lens paper. That was one reason he often left things places, because he was constantly freeing his hands for glasses polishing.

"I don't dare leave those stamps here where they might get stolen, Steve — someone may have gotten wind of 'em and followed me, for all I know — and I don't want to take 'em with me to the hospital, where anyone might lift 'em off me while I'm doped up or something. Nobody's safe any more!" Mr. Jonas declared bitterly, echoing the very words Steve's father had used at breakfast. "Now, don't you live out Sprague Park way?"

"Not far from it," said Steve. "In fact, I was going out there after I left here —"

"Heaven sent!" Mr. Jonas repeated with another eyeroll, then started as the sound of a siren reached their ears from the streets below. It approached, and stopped abruptly.

"That'll be the rescue squad coming now, so we don't have much time!" With an effort Mr. Jonas sat up on one elbow. "Now listen to me, boy. Mr. Kingsley Brant lives at Ten Brookside Drive, and that's on the other side of the park —"

"I know where it is."

"Good!" The old man fumbled in his pocket and brought out a small package. "Here they are, in their own special metal case, that's how valuable they are. Think you can take 'em to Mr. Brant for me, safe and sound?"

Steve hastily put on his glasses, and a package not more than two inches square wrapped in white paper and sealed with transparent tape came into focus. He gaped at it, but managed to say, "Sure I can!"

"What's that thing you're carrying?"

Glad to be reminded, Steve snatched up the case.

"It's got a kite in it."

"Hmm, Maybe . . . well, no, I don't know but what a pocket's best. Got a good safe pocket to put 'em in?"

"Yes, sir!"

"All right, then. And don't give 'em to anyone but Mr. Kingsley Brant, you hear? Now, if you'll do this for me, I'll let you have that Fugio Cent you're so crazy about" — and here the old man had a struggle, but finally managed to win out over his better self as he gasped — "for only ten dollars."

It would not have been like him to go all the way and *give* it to Steve, especially not when he happened to know he had ten dollars to spend. But even so, Mr. Jonas could hardly have come up with a more dazzling offer as far as Steve was concerned. Ten dollars! The Fugio Cent for ten dollars! And ten dollars he had!

He held out his hand for the package.

"Okay!"

Mr. Jonas gave it to him and watched him thrust it carefully into the right hand pocket of his slacks as deep as it would go.

"No holes in that pocket?"

"No, sir!"

"Got that name and address?"

"Mr. Kingsley Brant, Ten Brookside Drive."

"Good. Now get going, before anyone comes."

"But —"

"I'll be all right!" Mr. Jonas waved him impatiently on his way. "Git!"

Trembling with excitement, Steve obeyed. And he had no more than started up the corridor when at the far end elevator doors slid open and four men stepped out.

Two were in white uniforms and had a stretcher on wheels between them. The other men were in business suits. One was gray-haired and stocky, the other slim with dark hair and a thin face. As the ambulance men rolled the stretcher toward him, Steve pointed back to the office he had just left.

"Mr. Jonas is in there!"

"Thanks," said one of the men. The procession swept past him and entered the office.

Steve's natural impulse was to hang around and watch them wheel the patient out on the stretcher. But then he remembered what the old man had told him. If they brought him out and he saw Steve still hanging around, he'd probably be mad. "Git!" he had ordered, so Steve got.

He had already missed the elevator that had brought up the men. Its doors had closed and it was gone. Hurrying up the corridor, he pushed the elevator button and waited, taking advantage of the opportunity to polish his glasses, which were fogged over again from all the excitement. If they brought Mr. Jonas out now, he would at least see that Steve was on the job.

The stretcher did not reappear that quickly, however. Instead, one of the men stepped out into the corridor. The only thing Steve could be sure of at that distance, with his glasses off, was that it was not one of the ambulance men, because he was not in white. Otherwise he was a distant blur.

The elevator doors opened. Steve had all he could do to grab his kite case with his free hand and step inside. The doors closed, and he was alone.

He hoped he would have the elevator to himself all the way, but no such luck. It stopped at Four. A huge man stepped in, breathing as if he had been in a hurry. His belt buckle, square and steely, was on Steve's eye level. Steve looked up and saw at a great height an ape-jawed face that would have been at home in any Saturday night horror film. The monster bared his teeth and spoke in a soft voice that froze Steve's blood into jagged crystals.

"Hi, bud."

Steve gulped and squeaked out a "Hi!" Convulsively, before he could stop himself, his hand touched his pocket.

Now he had done it! Now he had given the whole show away! His heart almost stopped beating as the man asked, "What you got there, bud?"

"Nothing!"

He could not have picked a worse thing to say. Obviously, now, the man knew he was lying . . .

"You mean, that's a tube full of nothing?"

"Oh!"

Steve stared down at the kite case as though he were noticing it for the first time. He had forgotten he was carrying it.

"Oh, no, it's a kite! A collapsible kite!" cried Steve, looking fairly collapsible himself.

"A kite, is it? Well, you could have fooled me, bud."

Meanwhile the elevator had stopped at Three, and a little old lady joined them. Steve looked so pathetically glad to see her that she beamed at him and said, "Good morning, young man!"

"Good morning, ma'am."

"And what is your name?"

Steve darted his eyes at the belt buckle. A thousand TV crime shows, dredged up by his steel-trap memory and aided by his lively imagination, had already provided him with his motto for this unexpected adventure: trust nobody. Gulping again, he answered the old lady's question.

"Jimmie Smith, ma'am."

He was not about to give his real name at a time like this!

4

JIMMIE Smith? Now, that's a nice name," said the old lady, and he could feel his face heating up. Maybe it was only because he felt guilty, but he was sure she did not believe him.

By then the elevator was stopping at Two. Three more people got on. He began to breathe easier, even feel a little foolish. The feeling grew when they reached the ground floor and all the other passengers went their way without paying him the slightest heed. Even the monster walked off without a backward glance.

The only reason Steve did not follow them was that he had to stop and polish his glasses. When he had finished, he thought to check the floor indicators above the elevators. The arrow for the elevator next to his had stopped at five.

Was it stopping for Mr. Jonas? Again he was tempted to wait and see. Again, as the arrow started moving down, he decided he had better not. Instead he left the building, heading for the bus stop on the corner.

In front of the building the red rescue squad ambulance stood waiting, its red roof light revolving and its motor running. A crowd of curious onlookers waited on both sides of the entrance. It was much like the scenes he had watched so often on TV, and made his heartbeat pick up all over again. He was part of the action, and nobody knew it but himself — and Mr. Jonas, who was probably being brought down this very moment on a stretcher!

It was all Steve could do not to swagger. For that matter, it was hard to leave it all behind, but once again he remembered Mr. Jonas's instructions — and the Fugio Cent. He kept going till he reached the corner. Once there, he turned to watch. He was almost annoyed when he saw his bus was already coming, turning the corner into Main Street a block down. At this rate he would be gone before they even brought out Mr. Jonas.

Gripping his kite case on a slant between his knees, he reached for a lens paper. The packet of papers was in the same pocket with his special package. He transferred them to his left pocket, reserving the other one for its important contents, and took off his glasses to polish them.

The world turned fuzzy around him. When he glanced back at the Waverly Building, the man who came out of the entrance and stopped was a blurred figure, but something about him made Steve hurry to replace his glasses. The figure sharpened.

The man had dark hair and a thin face. Wasn't he the same one who had been with the ambulance men? And now he was glancing briefly but unmistakably in Steve's direction.

Worse yet, the bus had stopped now for a traffic light. Steve fidgeted nervously. Could it be that the man really was looking for him? What should he do if the man started walking his way?

Take off, that was what! Run! Find a policeman! Mr. Jonas had seemed afraid someone had "got wind of" the stamps. Maybe this was the man! What if he and the other man had been tailing Mr. Jonas, only to have their plans upset by the sudden appearance of the rescue squad? And then they had come upstairs with the ambulance men — any clever crook could think of some excuse for doing that. Could it be? . . .

But the man made no move. The light changed. The bus pulled up to Steve's corner. He leaped aboard, put his money in the box, miraculously avoided poking anyone with his kite case, and hurried to the back of the bus to check on his suspect.

The man was no longer in sight, but Steve stayed where he was, kneeling on the seat that ran across the back of the bus, looking out the rear window. He watched impatiently while a middle-aged couple came puffing up the street, waving for the bus to wait.

"Darn it, let's *go!*" he muttered to himself, but the bus waited. Not until they were on board did the doors finally hiss shut and the bus begin to move.

Only then did Steve turn and sit down to haul in a much-needed breath of air. He was being ridiculous, of course — that man was probably not after him at all — but for a moment back there Steve had felt like a rabbit being looked at by a fox. That was what the man's face had been like, a fox face. Steve was glad to leave him behind and be on his way, safe at last!

"Well, hello, Jimmie!"

He froze with his lungs full of air and went popeyed from the strain. Sitting beside him, smiling at him in a sweet way that scared him worse than the monster's grimace, was the old lady from the elevator.

"I almost missed the bus!" she told him in a cozy tone

of voice that only heightened his alarm. "I didn't expect it to come so soon, and I was in a shop up the street when here it came!"

A likely story!

A dozen TV crime shows he remembered all too clearly immediately suggested the truth about the sudden reappearance of this old lady. After all, she had stepped into the elevator only one floor below the one he had started from.

"Where are you going, Jimmie?"

There it was, right away — the key question!

"Home!" said Steve.

Home, and call the police! Call his friend Officer Joyce and get a police escort to Ten Brookside Drive! If there was one thing those crime shows had taught him, it was that you could not trust nice old ladies any more than anyone else. How many times had they been part of gangs, especially gangs of thieves?

She peered at him keenly over her spectacles.

"Home? And where is that, Jimmie?"

Now she was really trying to pump him!

"Why — uh — I live on Manton Avenue, ma'am," he told her.

Manton Avenue was two stops before his home stop, but that was where he now intended to get off. And then, if this old lady were really tailing him, trying to find out where he was going, she was out of luck. He would duck in through the front entrance of the dime store, out the back one, around the corner —

But . . . she wouldn't be working alone. She'd have help. Was someone else on the bus working with her? He shot wary glances at the other passengers, and at least half of them suddenly looked like hardened criminals. How about that couple who had come running to catch the bus at the last minute? Hadn't they come from the direction of the Waverly Building? . . .

"Where do you go to school, Jimmie?"

"Er — Mount Vernon, ma'am."

He remembered in the nick of time not to say Horace Mann. Manton Avenue kids didn't go to his school, they went to Mount Vernon.

"Mount Vernon? How nice! Then I'm sure you know little Bessie Alsop."

"B-Bessie Alsop? No, I don't think so."

"You don't? Now, that's odd, because Bessie must be just about your age."

Now she was trying to trap him!

"Well, I haven't been going there long," Steve decided to say. "I don't know all the kids yet."

"Oh, I see. Well, anyway, she's my grandniece, and I must tell her I met you."

The old lady peered out the window, then shifted her black purse from one hand to the other.

"It's been nice talking to you, Jimmie," she said, "but I have to get off now. I live in Bancroft House, and it's just lovely, but it's a bit too far for me to walk at my age, so I take the bus. Good-bye, Jimmie, and have a nice day!"

5

ONCE again Steve was feeling foolish.

He waved to the old lady when she stepped down from the bus, and gave himself a lecture. Just because he hated thieves so much, he was letting his imagination get the best of him. His imagination, liberally assisted by television, that is.

That poor old lady! There she went, thinking she had met a boy named Jimmie Smith who lived on Manton Avenue and went to Mount Vernon! Furthermore, one of these days she would confuse her grandniece Bessie Alsop by telling her about the boy she met from her school. He laughed out loud, then flushed and stared out the window as he realized some passengers across the aisle and one seat ahead had turned to look at him.

After a moment he glanced at them again — and now he saw who they were.

They were the same couple who had run to catch the bus!

Again his mind started spinning off a wild TV chase in which *they* were actually the ones who were following him, but this time he stopped himself short. Now, don't start *that* again, he told himself sternly. Those people sitting over there were ordinary people, just like that old lady —

But wait!

A clever old lady could have picked his pocket! She had been sitting close enough, and on his right side, too!

The thought jolted him upright in his seat. His hand flew to his pants leg, feeling for the bulge of the precious package.

It was gone!

Absolutely gone, and she was getting away while he sat there and —

No.

Wrong place.

When he was sitting, the package dropped down in his pocket, down against the seat. He had not felt in the right place. It was all right! He pressed the package hard against his leg, reveling in the comfort of knowing it was still there, safe and sound —

But was it?

On TV she would have taken it and slipped a dummy package in its place!

No, that was silly. Still, he could not rest easy until he had pulled the package up inside his pocket far enough to peer in and see a corner of it, and know it was unmistakably the one Mr. Jonas had given him.

And then, just in case anyone was watching him, he made a show of looking in his other pocket and bringing out a lens paper, as though that was what he had been searching for all the time.

He could still see the old lady, and she was certainly not hurrying anywhere. No black sedan had pulled up to the curb to whisk her away, none of that TV stuff. As he sat back trying to relax, he thought about how his father was always making fun of the crime shows until sometimes both Steve and his mother got mad and said, "Will you stop picking everything apart? You spoil the fun!"

Well, from now on Steve was going to be on his father's side, sneering at all that hooey!

Still . . . somebody *had* robbed the Craddock house only last night and grabbed a lot of furs and jewelry, and other people got robbed every day. It could happen. TV didn't make it *all* up.

Okay, he would be careful, and keep his eyes open, and not trust anybody, especially not Mame and George across the aisle there. He could hear them talking, and that was what they called each other. Mame and George. They couldn't have looked more harmless.

But . . . how about that old movie he had seen on TV only two nights ago, the one with James Stewart and Doris Day? They met a nice couple who looked as harmless as these people, and the first thing they knew the nice couple had kidnapped their little boy!

They had a dickens of a time getting him back.

What's more, they met those people on a bus, too.

Of course, they had been traveling in North Africa at the time, not riding out to Sprague Park. But it still showed you couldn't always go by people's looks.

What was more, in real life you didn't have any sinister music to tip you off. In a crime show, all they had to do was play some of that sinister music in the background and right away you knew the fox-faced man or the monster in the elevator or the little old lady or the harmless-looking couple were really dangerous crooks.

Steve grinned at the thought, and managed to relax a bit more. He told himself to stop worrying and making up things. The rest of his errand would be easy. All he

29

had to do was walk across Sprague Park, where there were lots of people around, and police cars patrolling the park, and where with any luck his special friend Officer Joyce would be on duty and at the wheel of his cruiser. No more than a mile across the park and he would be on Brookside Drive, knocking on the door of Number Ten.

He could almost visualize the houses. Mr. Brant must be rich if he lived there, because they were big houses set well apart with lots of trees and grass and flowers around them. Sprague Brook ran behind the houses on the south side of the street, which was the side Number Ten should be on. Come to think of it, that was why the street was named Brookside Drive.

After passing behind the houses, the brook ran into the park under Stimson Boulevard and eventually emptied into the lake in the center of the park. Steve knew that area, because once one of his kites, an Indian fighter kite, had caught in a tree near there, and he had not been able to get it down.

The bus was not crowded. Now that the old lady had gotten off he had the long back seat to himself. He laid the kite case on it beside him and began to make plans. After all, he did have a walk of nearly a mile ahead of him. Supposing, once he was in the park, he *did* get the feeling he was being followed? What would he do? How could he protect the stamps? How could he hide them?

He began to daydream, thinking up all sorts of melo-dramatic situations full of desperate crooks closing in on him, and wracking his brains for ways to foil them. He thought of one way that was so preposterous he laughed out loud again before he could stop himself. Once more Mame and George glanced around, once more he stared out the window, embarrassed. Even so, though, he continued to smile to himself. What a nutty idea!

After a moment his thoughts went to the Fugio Cent. At last he had time to think about it and get excited about actually having it in his collection.

He decided to make a surprise of it. Amy thought birthday presents should be surprises. All right, this present would be a surprise — only this time it would be the givers who got the surprise!

He would put his Fugio Cent in one of the clear plastic envelopes collectors used to protect coins, and he would put the envelope in a box and give it to his mother to wrap.

Then, on the morning of his birthday, he would tear off the wrappings, take the envelope out of the box, and show it to them without saying a word.

He could well imagine some of the things *they* would say:

"Well, what's this? It looks pretty old . . ."

"Hey!" (This from Amy, of course.) "It says 'Fugio' and '1787'!"

"Yes, and 'Mind Your Business.' Steve!" (Father staring at son, alarmed.) "Isn't this —"

"Yes." (Steve sitting back, very cool.) "It's the Fugio Cent."

"What? But you said it cost thirty dollars!"

"It does."

Then, and only then, when they were all popeyed, would he finally tell them the story of how he got it. . . .

Past Manton Avenue rode Steve, lost in happy daydreams — daydreams which, in this case, would actually come true if he could complete his mission successfully for Mr. Jonas.

He felt the package in his pocket again and began to look forward to the moment when he would hand it over to Mr. Brant and be free of responsibility. What a treat it would be then to run back to the park without a care in the world and spend the rest of the morning trying out his new kite!

The bus stopped at his own corner, but Steve was still dreaming blank-eyed out the window and paid no attention. So it came as a surprise, and not a pleasant one, when a greeting yanked him back into the present.

"Hi, Steve!"

He blinked, and saw a schoolmate coming down the aisle toward him, all silly grin and loud mouth.

Sticky Stoneham. Steve almost groaned. Ordinarily he did not mind Sticky as much as most of the kids did, because with all his faults Sticky was a fellow coin collector, and a pretty shrewd one. But right now there were few people Steve could have done without more easily than Sticky Stoneham.

"You going to the park? So am I!" Sticky trumpeted the good news as he bounced down on the seat next to Steve, peering past him at the kite case. "Hey, what's that funny-looking can?"

"What do you mean, funny-looking?" snapped its creator.

"Looks like something that ought to be in orbit," was Sticky's opinion. "What you got in it, Steve?"

"A kite."

"A kite? Must be in tough shape."

"It's a collapsible kite, you dope!"

"No kidding!" said Sticky, resorting to his favorite expression. "You going to fly it, Steve? I'll come along and watch."

Steve squirmed every time Sticky called him by name. George had glanced around. Steve saw him say something to Mame. Had they heard the old lady call him Jimmie? Were they wondering why Sticky was calling him by a different name? Of course, if they were just an ordinary, harmless couple, it didn't matter. But all the same . . .

"Hey, how come you were already on the bus, Steve? Where you been?"

"Downtown."

"No kidding! Did you see old Jonas?"

Steve was squirming again. How could he deny it? If by some wild chance Mame and George *were* crooks who had followed him, then they already knew he had been to see Mr. Jonas. The best thing to do was talk naturally, as if he had nothing to hide. So he said, "Yes, I went up to see him about getting a couple of things my family said I could have for my birthday, and guess what, Sticky?"

"What?"

"He was sick, and he had to be taken to the hospital!"

"No kidding! What was wrong with him?"

"Ulcers."

"Ulcers, huh? Like my Uncle Herman. Boy, is he a grouch! Well, did you buy anything?"

"How could I buy anything? He was too sick. They took him to the hospital while I was still there."

"No kidding! Gee, I wish I'd been there," grumbled Sticky, who hated to miss any excitement.

That ought to hold him, thought Steve, feeling pretty good about his handling of the conversation. He had not given one thing away, and it was a pleasure to think about how much Sticky *didn't* know. Not that Steve was really worried about Mame and George, when it came to that, but still . . . Each time the bus stopped he hoped they would get off, just to relieve his mind.

But they stayed on, and before long the park was in sight, and it was plain they were going all the way. Well, there was nothing so unusual about anyone going out to the park on a nice day. And yet . . .

Even if they went their own way without paying any attention to him, he would still have the problem of figuring some way to shake off Sticky, because he did not want him tagging along all the way to Mr. Brant's house. And shaking off Sticky would not be easy. When he found out you were going to fly a kite and he said, "I'll come along and watch," that was not a suggestion, it was a statement of fact.

He had not gained his nickname for nothing — and incidentally, he had never seemed to mind it, maybe because his real name was Elwood. Sticky Stoneham, the Flypaper Kid, they called him at Horace Mann. Ever since he was old enough to walk he had been the kind of pest who followed other kids wherever they went even when they didn't want him around, which was most of the time. If Sticky Stoneham decided he was going to come along and watch Steve fly his kite, it would take some pretty tricky maneuvering to get rid of him.

The bus rumbled forward and swung around the circle in front of the park entrance.

"Come on, Steve," said Sticky. "Hey, want me to carry that thing?"

"No! I'll carry it."

34

Steve took his time picking up his kite case. He pretended to check the hook and eye that held the cap shut.

"What's the matter, Steve?"

"I just want to make sure it's shut tight."

"I don't blame you. Looks like it could pop open on you any minute. Where did you buy that kooky outfit?"

"I made it myself!"

"Might have known," sighed Sticky.

By now Mame and George were where Steve wanted them, standing in front of the door, waiting to get off. He followed Sticky forward and stood in the aisle behind him.

George glanced around casually.

"Say, young fellow, do you really have a kite in there?"

Steve hoped his face did not look as taut as it suddenly felt. He nodded jerkily.

"Yes, sir."

"What kind?"

"Why — uh — it's a triangular box kite."

"Hmm." George glanced at Mame. "Say, that's something I'd like to see. I used to be a great kite flyer myself when I was a boy. What say we go along and watch?"

Mame glanced sharply at Steve, and shrugged. "I don't mind."

Steve's mouth had gone dry. If anyone had asked him, he would have sworn he could hear sinister music somewhere in the background. The kind of music they played on TV when they wanted you to know there was dirty work afoot.

6

THE sinister music stopped, however, almost as soon as it began. Even for a nervous boy with TV on the brain, Mame and George simply did not fill the bill. Mame looked like the kind of woman who would start talking about cake mixes at the drop of a hat. George had the big, pink, open face of an overgrown schoolboy. He *looked* like the kind of man who would want to watch a boy fly his kite.

But even if they were harmless, they were still a nuisance, they and Sticky Stoneham. Because now, instead of being able to take off and hotfoot it across the park straight to Brookside Drive, Steve found himself leading a parade of pests who expected him to fly a kite.

What could he do? It would be torture to have to stop and spend time flying it, with that package burning in his pocket the whole time. But unless he could think of some way to shake loose from these three, he would have no other choice.

"Where do you fly kites out here?" asked George. "Is it very far?"

"Naw!" said Sticky helpfully, "we'll be there in no time."

George sniffed the air and looked up at the sky.

"Good day for it. Plenty of wind," he said, which was

true. Ordinarily on such a day Steve would have been hurrying ahead, eager to get at it.

"Steve's the best kite flyer in our whole school!" declared Sticky.

"That so? Say, we've got a nephew in your school. You go to Mount Vernon, don't you?"

"Mount Vernon? Heck, no!" said Sticky, scorning the thought. "We go to Horace Mann!"

Steve felt his face heat up as George stopped dead in his tracks and stared down at him.

"Oh? That's funny, I thought I heard you tell that old lady on the bus you went to Mount Vernon."

They had all stopped now, and Mame was staring at him too, not to mention Sticky.

"Yes, what's with you, anyway?" asked Mame. "She called you Jimmie, and now this boy calls you Steve."

The situation was too much for Steve. He could not think up any pat answers to get him off the hook. Longing to clobber Sticky, he glared at him through fogged-up glasses, then did the best he could.

"She must have had me mixed up with some other kid. I was feeling silly, so I made up answers to her questions."

Mame was indignant. She gave him a scolding.

"Well, I never! A fine way to treat a nice old lady!"

"I know, I wish now I hadn't done it," said Steve truthfully.

"I wish I'd been there," said Sticky.

"You ought to be ashamed of yourself — and don't you laugh at him, George! If you ask me, I don't think we should have anything more to do with a boy who acts like that!"

A chance to get rid of them! Steve was quick to hang his head and say, "You're right, ma'am. We'll go away. Come on, Sticky —"

But good old George was chuckling tolerantly.

"Listen, I used to do things like that when I was a boy, too, just for the fun of it. Devil gets into you sometimes."

"George Benson, don't you start talking about what a rowdy you were when *you* were a boy, you'll only encourage them!"

"Okay, dear — but I want to see that kite of his, so stop picking on him and come on."

"Well . . . all right, but I don't approve," grumbled Mame, and Steve was still stuck with them.

"There's the meadow," said Sticky, pointing as they started walking again.

Ahead of them the park opened out into a wide, flat expanse of grass with flower beds lining the paths around it, and with a park road bounding it on the far side, separating it from the woods beyond. Steve let Sticky carry his case while he polished his glasses. They were badly in need of attention after all he had been through.

"Oh, yes, I remember now," said George. "We've only been out here once before, but I remember this now. Great place to put up a kite."

"There's a whole bunch of kite nuts out here every Sunday," said Sticky.

"I'll bet there are. Well, now, let's see that kite of yours, Steve. I'm curious to know how you pack one in a thing like that."

Resigned to his fate, Steve checked the wind.

"I'd better put her up from the other side of the meadow," he said, and led the way across the grass. Not far from the road he stopped, checked the wind again, and laid his kite case on the ground.

If his new kite performed properly, he should be able to pay it out from his hand, standing still, and put it up. George would enjoy that. Then, once it was up, they would probably not hang around long.

After they were gone he would figure out some way to get free of Sticky. If worst came to worst, he would tell Sticky he had to go see someone for a minute, and would ask him to fly the kite while he was gone.

But Sticky would probably manage to wreck it before he got back. There ought to be a better way!

He went down on his knees beside the case. With his father's help he had made a hinged cap for one end of the tube, with a hook and eye to hold it shut. He was pushing the hook out of the eye when the sound of a car motor idling along made him look up.

Suddenly he saw deliverance coming his way. Not only was it a police cruiser, but his friend was at the wheel.

"Hey, there's Officer Joyce! I've been wanting to see him and tell him something!" Steve snapped the hook shut and scrambled to his feet, taking his kite case with him. "Just a minute, I'll be right back!"

George looked surprised but not concerned. Mame sniffed impatiently and said, "George, I'm going over there and sit down. My feet hurt!"

As for Sticky, Steve knew he could count on his staying put. Sticky wanted no part of this particular policeman ever since Officer Joyce had caught him throwing stones at ducks in the lake and had almost run him in.

At first, as Steve raced toward the cruiser waving his free arm like some desert island castaway who had sighted a ship, he had no plan in mind. He simply felt Officer

Joyce could be of help in some way. By the time the car had stopped and he had reached it, however, an idea had occurred to him.

"Hi, there, Steve. What's up?"

"I've got to see you!"

Steve ran around the front of the car to the driver's side.

"What's the matter, Steve? What have you got there? That the new kite you were telling me about?"

Officer Joyce knew him as a kite nut, and had often watched him do his stuff there in the meadow.

"Yes, it is — but listen!" Panting a little, looking very earnest and owlish behind his big glasses, Steve lowered his voice to a confidential murmur. "I'm trying to get away from Sticky Stoneham. I've got an errand to do, and I don't want him tagging along."

Even though he had entertained some panicky notions about asking for a police escort back there on the bus when he was letting that nice old lady make him so nervous, it was quite a different matter to be actually talking to a police officer. Not in a thousand years could he have gotten up his nerve, face to face, to ask Officer Joyce to drive him to a house a few blocks away. For one thing, he no longer felt in any danger. That being the case, he had no intention of admitting he ever *had* felt in any danger. All he had to do now was get clear of Sticky Stoneham and he could be on Brookside Drive in ten minutes' time on his own two feet.

Behind them, across the road, the ground dropped off into a wooded area that extended all the way to the edge of the park. Steve spoke urgently to his friend.

"Will you sit here for a minute and let me sneak across the road and run down into the woods?"

"Oh, I get it! You want a shield, huh?"

"Yes!"

A hundred yards up the road a taxicab that had stopped beside the meadow started up and came toward them. The officer grinned at Steve.

"Sure, Steve, why not? I can't wait to see Sticky's face when I pull away and you're gone." He glanced in his side mirror and cautioned, "Get moving, there's a car coming."

Ducking low, Steve scooted across the road and plunged down the hillside, his arms out for balance, his kite case swinging recklessly. In a matter of seconds he was among the trees and traveling fast, with only a few minor stumbles.

Once he was deep in the woods, completely hidden from the road, he stopped to listen. He heard nothing. All around him there was only blessed silence and tall trees, with a butterfly or two fluttering around some low bushes, and sunlight slanting through the green leaves above him.

A moment passed while he stood catching his breath. Then in the distance he heard a shrill cry.

"Steve! Hey, Steve!"

It was Sticky. Steve wanted to snicker, but stopped himself. Time to get moving again. If he knew Sticky, he would be on his trail in short order. And long years of practice had made Sticky very good at nosing out people. Steve started on again, walking as quietly as possible.

As quietly as possible for him, that is. Steve was not much of a nature boy. On hikes, on the few occasions he had been unable to avoid them, he had always seemed to be the one who got a stone in his shoe, or blundered into a nest of yellow jackets, or brained himself against a low branch. Small rustling sounds made him uneasy; he was always sure they were made by snakes, and was never

eager to investigate. But this was one time he was happy to find himself alone in the woods.

Before long his trail crossed a bridle path. Steve turned and followed it without a moment's hesitation. He was pretty sure the path came out close to the Stimson Boulevard entrance to the park. And that entrance was directly across from Brookside Drive.

He had followed the path up a slope that swung it near a park road when he heard the sound of a motor approaching. Since there was no point in taking any unnecessary chances, he dropped down flat beside a bush to let the car go past.

The car turned out to be a taxicab.

It was moving very slowly, and its passenger was sitting beside the window, peering out.

Steve's heart thumped against the ground. The man was wearing dark glasses now, but they were not enough of a disguise to leave any doubt in Steve's mind.

Fox Face!

It was the same man. The one who had appeared with the rescue squad, the one who had come out of the building and looked around while he was waiting for the bus.

The cab rolled slowly past, and Steve was left with a brand new world, a world in which the menace was no longer imaginary, no longer TV make-believe.

Now it was real, and dangerously close.

7

UP TO that moment, no matter how frightened he had felt, there had been a voice in the back of Steve's mind saying, "Aw, cut it out! This isn't TV, this is real life! You've got robbers on the brain!"

Now that voice was gone. In its place was a lonely new sensation that made the air seem to grow crystal clear around him, made every leaf and tree and blade of grass stand out, made even the slightest sound come through loud and clear in that heightening of the senses only actual danger produces.

This, then, was how it really felt, this heart-pounding alertness. Was this the way the rabbit felt when he watched the fox trot by, sniffing the wind but missing the scent?

He could understand what had happened, and how simple it all had been. The man had simply gotten into a cab and followed the bus, and then tailed him into the park.

Steve's first impulse was to run straight back to Officer Joyce. But by now he would be gone, making his rounds. The meadow would offer only large open spaces, exposed and dangerous. For the rabbit, the woods were safer.

He sat up and felt the hard outlines of the package in his pocket with something like awe. How valuable *were* those stamps, anyway? They must be worth plenty. But wait a minute! *Why* was Fox Face following him? When you stopped to think about it, a man could hardly jump out of a taxicab in broad daylight and pounce on a boy and take a package away from him while the cabdriver was sitting there watching. That could hardly be what he had in mind.

The sensation of immediate danger lessened as new possibilities occurred to him. If this Mr. Brant could buy a set of stamps like these, then his collection was probably worth a fortune. Maybe *that* was what they were after!

Maybe Fox Face was tailing him because he wanted to find out who could buy those stamps, and then go after his whole collection! Like the gang that broke into the Craddocks' house because they knew they would find a lot of furs and jewelry.

But what had made Fox Face suspect he was delivering the stamps to someone for Mr. Jonas?

Steve thought back, starting in Mr. Jonas's office, and soon his face reddened.

Of course!

He had made two bad mistakes.

First, when those men had come striding down the hall, what had he done? He had pointed back and told them, "Mr. Jonas is in there!"

How could he have known that if he hadn't just been in there with Mr. Jonas himself?

Secondly, when ambulance men came down a hall with a stretcher and took it into an office, what would any normal kid do?

He would hang around to watch the excitement. Take Sticky, now; you couldn't have dragged him away with wild horses till he had watched them bring Mr. Jonas out.

But what had Steve done? He had told them where the sick man was and then gone straight to the elevator. And while he was waiting for it, one of those men, probably Fox Face, had come out and looked up the hall at him.

He might as well have carried a sign saying, "I've got the stamps!"

He had done it all wrong, but now by sheer good luck he had thrown the fox off the scent, and now the important thing was to get to Ten Brookside Drive without being seen. But how? If he stayed in the woods till he reached the wall at the edge of the park and then climbed the wall, he would still have to expose himself crossing the boulevard, not to mention walking to the corner and turning up Brookside Drive to Number Ten.

"Hey, Steve!"

It was Sticky again, somewhere in the distance. Not too much distance, either. All he needed now was for Sticky Stoneham to find him and start blabbing questions in his loud voice. He ought to get moving, but where could he —

The culvert!

He was thankful he had lost that Indian fighter kite in a tree near the brook, because suddenly he remembered the culvert.

There was still a fair amount of water in the brook at that time of year, early in the summer, but not enough to matter. It wouldn't be more than knee deep. He could wade through the culvert, keep going along the brook, and come up *behind* the houses on Brookside Drive. That way he would not be seen crossing the boulevard. It was easy. Straight ahead through the woods to the wall, then along beside the wall till he came to the brook and the culvert.

Standing up carefully, but staying low, Steve stopped, looked, and listened. Silence. No cars were coming. No crackle of twigs suggested the footsteps of Sticky Stoneham closing in on him.

Skittering across the bridle path, Steve plunged into the woods again.

There was only one trouble with the Sprague Park woods. They were real woods.

They were dense, and rapidly grew more so. Before long it became a struggle just to make headway, especially for a boy who tended to stumble over things and who was further hampered by a three-foot tubular kite case.

If only he had left it at home! But how was he to know he would become involved in a crazy errand that would find him plowing through woods before he was finished?

Now he wished he had gone on more hikes, and had paid more attention to learning some woods lore the times he had gone. If he had, he could now stash his kite case somewhere and come back for it later. But he knew himself well enough to know he would never find it again if he did.

So on he went, dragging the thing along, and it was a wonder the case survived the trip at all. When he wasn't bumping it against a tree trunk he was banging it against his kneecaps.

Several times he went sprawling, because if there was a root concealed anywhere in the undergrowth, his feet unerringly found it. A large beetle with a hard shell and a great many scratchy legs could think of nothing better to do than drop down the back of his neck and then try to claw its way out, while Steve did a war dance and all but stood on his head.

He could find his way through city streets without a hitch, but when he was in the woods he did not have much sense of direction, nor much knowledge as to how to keep directions straight. He struggled on for a long time without any sign of a wall coming his way. After a while he knew he was completely turned around and lost.

Hoping to get his bearings, he spotted a small clearing and made for it. But just as he was stepping into it, one more root decided to have some fun with him. He tumbled forward with such force his glasses flew off when he hit the ground.

He was so infuriated he grumbled out loud.

"Darn these woods!" he muttered. "I hate them!"

He was pawing the ground for his glasses, hoping they were not broken, when half a dozen shadowy shapes, silent as Indians, rose up at the far edge of the little clearing.

"Got him!"

"He's the one!"

"Shut up, Randy!"

8

AT THAT instant Steve's hand touched his glasses. He snatched them up and put them on. The shapes resolved themselves into boys in Scout uniforms, and an unfriendlier bunch of Scouts he had never seen. They were all bigger and older than he was, of course. A tall boy who had Eagle Scout and Leader written all over his commanding countenance stepped into the clearing, followed by the others. He glowered down at Steve.

"What have you got there?"

Steve stared up at him, bewildered, then realized what he was talking about.

"Oh! This? It's a kite."

Hoots and jeers greeted this statement.

"A kite! That's a hot one!"

"I'd like to see anyone fly *that!*"

"Hey, we've got a real nut on our hands!"

"Well, what did you expect? He'd have to be nutty to —"

Their leader held up a stern hand for silence.

"What do you mean, a kite?"

"Well, it is!"

"Let's see it."

Steve glanced resentfully around the circle of faces.

"Listen, I'm in a big hurry, and — Okay, okay, I'll

show you!" he decided hastily as they all took a threatening step toward him.

Carefully, grudgingly, he opened the case, pulled the folded box kite out of its tube, and unfolded it sufficiently for them to see it was unquestionably a kite.

"Hey, what do you know?"

"It really is a kite!"

"Sure, but that doesn't prove anything," said one skeptic with a squeaky voice. "It could still be a cover-up for whatever else he's got in there."

Glaring at them now, Steve brought out the rest of his equipment. When he emptied the tube, he held it up for them to see, and complained bitterly.

"What's the big idea? Some Scouts you guys are, the whole bunch of you picking on one kid!"

Their leader resented this suggestion, so alien to Scouting principles.

"Nobody's picking on you," he retorted stiffly. "We've got good reasons for wanting to know what you're up to."

"And not only that," said the squeaky voice, "since when does anybody sneak into the woods to fly a kite?"

"Shut up, Randy!" ordered the leader automatically, and then had second thoughts about it. "Well, yes, that's a point. What *are* you doing here with a kite?"

"I've got good reasons too!"

"Such as what?"

"Well . . ."

That was an interesting question, of course. But how much should he tell?

"Well, I'm doing a good deed," said Steve, deciding that might be his best approach.

Best or not, it was hardly the sort of reply the Scouts had been expecting. They exchanged surprised glances.

"What do you mean, a good deed?"

Steve took a deep breath.

"Well, there's this old man who's sick, see?"

"So?"

"So he asked me to take something to somebody, and I'm doing it, and I've got to get there as quick as I can," he said, keeping it cryptic.

Maybe he was too cryptic. At any rate, he only succeeded in setting off a new round of jeers.

"Oh, boy!"

"Wow!"

"If that's what you're doing, what are you doing here? Nobody lives in the park!"

"He thinks he's Little Red Riding Hood walking through the woods to Grandmother's House!"

By now Steve's face was beet red. "I was just taking a short cut!" he snapped.

This was so preposterous it silenced them all for a few seconds. Then:

"A *short* cut?" said their leader.

"This guy really is nuts, Smitty!"

"He's right off his rocker!"

Steve was ready to give up. But then he thought, if you can't lick 'em, join 'em. Ask them for help. After all, that was what Scouts were supposed to be: helpful.

He spread his arms in an appeal to Smitty, their leader. "Listen!"

Smitty eyed him grimly.

"We're listening."

"I'll tell you the whole thing," stalled Steve, trying to get his words together.

"Okay, tell us."

"Well, I was trying to get to Sprague Brook, but I got lost."

"You got *lost?* In *these* woods?"

Smitty glanced around in grand disdain, unable to comprehend such a thing, while Steve reddened again.

"I had a lot on my mind, and I got turned around!" he declared. "But anyway, if you'll help me get to the brook I'll *show* you what I mean by a short cut. Do you know where the brook is from here?"

The question was almost too much for Smitty.

"Do we know where the brook is from here! Listen, we know these woods backwards and forwards —"

"And sideways!"

"And even if we didn't we could still find the brook with our eyes shut. I didn't get my Hiking Badge for nothing."

"Well, then —"

"Not so fast. Don't think you can get away that easy!"

"He's the one, Smitty!"

"Sure he is!"

"*What* one? What are you talking about? What did you think I had in there, anyway?" asked Steve, pointing to his kite case.

Once again glances shot from Scout to Scout.

"Well . . ."

"Incendiary materials!" cried the squeaky voice.

"Randy, will you shut up?"

"What's he talking about?" demanded Steve.

"Don't try to act innocent," snapped Smitty. "We all heard what you said."

"What do you mean, what I said?"

"You said you hated the woods."

"When? Oh!" Steve remembered. "You mean, when I fell down? Well, sure, but that was only because I was trying to hurry and —"

Incendiary materials? Stuff to start a fire with? . . .

"Hey! You mean, you thought I was going to start a fire in the woods?"

Now, at last, Steve understood. And now he was outraged.

"For Pete's sake, why would I want to do a thing like that?"

His honest indignation had its effect on Smitty.

"Well, you might," he said. "Didn't you hear about yesterday?"

"What about yesterday?"

"Some firebug tried to a set a fire in the woods yesterday. So when we saw you come sneaking along carrying that weird gizmo —"

"Weird gizmo?" cried its insulted creator.

"It's a funny-looking thing to be carrying in the woods," insisted Smitty. "You could have anything in it."

"Well, you've got the wrong guy. I don't even have a pack of matches with me, and you can search me if you want to!" declared Steve, throwing his arms out at his sides in a fine fit of righteous anger.

And just as abruptly he dropped them, as he suddenly remembered what he did have in his pocket.

His change of expression was enough to stir suspicions all over again.

"What's the matter?" asked Smitty.

"He looks funny to me!" squeaked Randy.

"He's hiding something!"

"Frisk him!"

Steve quickly faced facts. Matters were getting completely out of hand. The time had come when there was nothing to do but lay his cards on the table.

"Now, wait a minute! I *am* hiding something. I *told* you I was taking something to someone for that sick old man. It's very valuable, too, and that's why I'm sneaking through the woods, because I was afraid a man was following me, and I don't want him to find out where I'm taking it."

He pulled the small package out of his pocket and flourished it dramatically.

"Here, this is what I'm carrying!"

They all stared.

"Well . . . what is it?" asked Smitty.

"Can you keep a secret?"

"Sure!"

"Okay. It's a set of valuable stamps."

"You mean postage stamps?"

"Yes."

"Where did you get them?"

"From Mr. Jonas that runs the Jonas Coin and Stamp Company."

"I know him," one Scout declared. "I've bought stamps from him myself."

"Well, he's the one. When I went to his office this morning he was sick and had to go to the hospital, so he asked me to deliver these for him, because he was afraid to leave them in his office. And the house I'm heading for is over on Brookside Drive, so I figured the way I could get there without anyone seeing me was to come through the woods and sneak through the culvert!"

There was silence for a moment. The boys stared at him

woodenly, and Steve's heart sank. He was sure none of them believed him. But then —

"Well, why didn't you say so in the first place?" snorted Smitty. "Put your stuff back in that gizmo and let's get going!"

9

THE Scouts did the job. Steve suffered the humiliation of being led to a trail not twenty yards away which was almost as well marked as the bridle path. It brought them to Sprague Brook near the culvert in less than five minutes.

Nevertheless, Steve was grateful.

"I'll be on the meadow flying my kite Sunday, if you want to hear how I made out today."

"I'll look for you," said Smitty. "Sure you don't want us to guard you the rest of the way?" he added wistfully. Chances like this one did not come along every day in the lives of a Scout patrol.

"No, I don't need a guard, I just need to not be seen," Steve pointed out. "So I'm better off alone."

"Huh! I'm not so sure," said Smitty. "Still, I guess even you won't get lost again when all you have to do is follow a brook. But listen. When you get old enough, you'd better join the Scouts and learn something. You sure are dumb when it comes to being out in the woods."

Steve's face heated up again.

"I'll think about it," he promised.

The culvert was a tube of concrete some seven or eight feet in diameter. As he had expected, the flow of water through it was about knee deep. He rolled up the legs of

his slacks, stepped carefully into the brook, waved back at the Scouts, and started toward the culvert, holding his kite case high. Behind him the squeaky voice offered a final comment.

"I still think he's a nut!"

"Shut up, Randy!" Steve growled under his breath, and stepped into the concrete tube.

Cool and swift-flowing, the water dragged at his feet and swirled about his knees, making each step an effort. The culvert set up a hollow rumble around him as traffic passed on the road overhead. When he neared the center of the tube, the wet, slimy walls glistened darkly around him. Underground chases he had seen on TV inevitably came to mind, including one from an old movie about a man fleeing through the sewers of Paris, but oddly enough instead of being scared he felt light-hearted and excited, and sort of pleased with himself. He almost had to pinch himself to realize this was the real thing.

Fox Face would be surprised to know where he was now!

Poor old Mr. Jonas would be surprised, too. But at least he would have to admit Steve was earning his Fugio Cent.

Steve's eyes flashed in the gloom as he struggled along. It gave him fierce pleasure to think he was outwitting a gang of thieves. When he got a chance to tell his story to Mr. Brant and the police, maybe something could be done to find out who they were and set a trap for them. But whatever happened, he would have a story to tell! He could see himself now, lolling back in his chair at home, being very cool and casual as he told his family all about it.

But that could wait. Right now he had to plan what he was going to do when he left the culvert.

Fortunately both banks of the brook were lined with

trees. If he stayed along the bank, he could go the rest of the way under cover.

When he reached the end of the culvert he stopped to listen carefully for traffic sounds above him on the boulevard. Between the end of the culvert and the first trees on that side of the road there was a space of about ten feet or so that offered no cover. Anyone who happened to look down from a car might be able to see him. He decided to wait till he could not hear any cars coming before he exposed himself.

There was good footing, almost a path, along the right bank. As soon as there was a lull in the traffic overhead, he stepped out of the culvert and edged sideways to the bank. He listened again, twitching like a rabbit, then made a run for the cover of the trees.

A few steps, and one slight slip, and he was out of sight. Once more he stopped to listen. Now a car or two were coming, now several more. But they were all moving fast. None slowed down on the way past. He peered up through the trees, whose leaves were still fluttering in a good breeze. No car was parked near the culvert. He turned and went on.

The path, if it had been one, disappeared. The footing became tricky along the edge of the bank, but he hurried ahead. He was in a fever now to get there and be done with it. How far along would Number Ten be?

He stared up the bank again through the trees and caught a glimpse of a rooftop nearby. That would be the first house.

Since the houses were not jammed together, but had large yards around them, they would probably not be numbered two, four, six, eight, ten, like smaller houses. Maybe the next one would be Number Ten, or at most the one after that. Anyway, he would go at least one house farther before he cut up into the backyards and looked for someone who could give him directions.

He was picking his way around an especially difficult spot, where a tree trunk jutted down the bank, when a deep voice startled him.

"Hello, sonny. Where are you going?"

He jerked his head up to see who had spoken, and took a step forward at the same time.

It was the wrong moment to look away. His foot swung squarely into the loop of a root, the root gave it a vicious twist, and he stumbled sideways into the brook.

Splashing and thrashing, he half fell into the water before he found his feet. When he did find them he could hardly stand on them. His glasses were spattered, and his kite case had a dent in it from banging against a rock.

Footsteps scrabbled down the bank onto brookside pebbles. He had a watery vision of large hands reaching out to him. With their help he hobbled ashore.

The man who had helped him was a tall man with wavy blond hair and large blue eyes.

"Sorry, kid, I didn't mean to scare you. Did you hurt yourself?"

Steve lifted his right foot and winced at the pain.

"My ankle hurts."

Another man appeared at the edge of the lawn above the bank.

"Hey, Arnie, what happened?"

"It's okay, Fred. This boy fell in the brook. What's your name, kid?"

"Steve O'Neill."

"Well, Steve, let's get you up on dry land and have a look at that ankle."

Arnie picked him up, climbed the bank on sturdy legs, and sat him on the grass of a large, well-kept lawn under a big shade tree. Hunching down in front of him, he untied Steve's wet sneaker, pulled it off, and touched the swollen ankle.

"You did a job on it, all right. Better get an ice pack on that. You live around here, Steve?"

"No."

"Just walking the brook, huh?"

"Well, no. I'm looking for somebody who lives around here."

"Oh? Who?"

"Mr. Kingsley Brant."

The men exchanged a glance, and Arnie laughed.

"Well, you've got to give him credit, Fred, he came to the right place."

"Is this Ten Brookside Drive?"

"It sure is. But you certainly did it the hard way, Steve. This place is a lot easier to find if you just walk up the street."

For an instant Steve experienced a miniature version of what Columbus must have felt when he finally sighted land. He had made it! But his pleasure was as quickly chilled by uncertainties. Who were these men? He still had to be careful.

"Well, I was trying to sneak away from another boy. I didn't want him tagging along."

He knew that sounded like kid stuff, but he didn't care. So much the better. He wiped his glasses on his shirt front and pulled out a lens paper.

Arnie was grinning at him.

"Well, anyway, here you are. You're right in Mr.

Brant's backyard. Fred and I work for him. He's out just now, but he'll be back shortly. What's on your mind? Anything we can take care of?"

Still cautious, Steve sought for words.

"Well . . . no. It's something I'm supposed to see him about personally."

Arnie pursed his lips and nodded.

"Personally, huh? Well, okay then, we'll take you in and get you fixed up with an ice pack and you can wait for him. He shouldn't be long. He's just gone to bring home a sofa that's being reupholstered."

Arnie picked up Steve again with the greatest of ease. He was impressively muscular, and in better shape than Fred. Fred was a heavy-jawed man with lots of beef that was running to lard, especially around his middle. He had the face of a retired boxer who had lost most of his fights.

"Bring his sneaker, Fred, and that tube," said Arnie. "What have you got in that thing, anyway?"

"A kite."

"A kite? Well, how about that? You mean one you can take apart and fold up and stuff in there?"

"Yes. It's a triangular box kite. I made it myself. I made the case, too."

"Say, you're really something. I want to see that kite, it must be a pip."

The house was a long, one-story modern one. They crossed the lawn toward the back door. Fred held it open for them. Arnie carried Steve through a bright kitchen and down a hall to a bedroom.

"This is my room." He lowered Steve into an over-stuffed armchair and pushed a footstool in front of the chair. "Put your foot up on that. I'll go fill Fred's ice bag. That'll make it feel better."

"Thanks."

Steve's ankle was throbbing, but sitting quietly with his leg up made the pain lessen. Fred came in, tossed his sneaker on the floor beside him, and leaned his kite case against the chair, all without a word. Fred did not seem to be the talkative type.

Steve looked at the case and saw a drop of water running down its side.

"Please, could you hand me that?" he asked anxiously. "I want to make sure no water got inside."

Fred managed to grunt out a reply.

"Okay."

He laid the case across Steve's lap and left. Steve opened it and found his fears confirmed. Some water had gotten inside; not a lot, but enough to make it necessary to pull everything out for a thorough examination.

The Zephyrlite kite cloth could take some moisture, but the less the better, of course. He decided the best way to make sure the kite dried quickly would be to put it together, so that air could get to all parts of the cloth. Besides, that would give him a chance to show it off to Arnie, who had said he would like to see it.

He was assembling the kite when Arnie returned with the ice bag.

"Well! So that's the production, is it?"

Steve explained why he was putting it together.

"Good idea." Arnie draped the ice bag on Steve's ankle. "How's that?"

"Feels great!"

"It's Fred's lifesaver for his kind of headaches, I can

tell you that," said Arnie with a slightly malicious grin. He glanced around and pointed to the portable television set that faced the armchair. "Well, how about some entertainment? Want to see what's on the tube?"

Steve shook his head.

"No, thanks. It's all junk at this time of day."

"I expect you're right." Arnie turned toward a table cluttered with record albums lying beside a player. "How about some music?"

"Sure. Anything but the Lowest Common Denominators," added Steve.

"You don't like them, huh?"

"No, but my sister does. She plays their stuff all the time."

Arnie held up an album.

"Here's their newest one. I just got it, and I'm on your side. It stinks. Here, you take it to her for a present."

"Gee, thanks! She'll be glad to get it!"

Arnie watched Steve finish assembling the kite, then put it aside for him on the bed.

"You can leave it there till you go. When Mr. Brant comes back with the car and you get your personal business taken care of, I'll run you home."

Arnie kept his face perfectly straight when he said "personal business," but Steve had a feeling he was making fun of him. He had a hunch Arnie knew why he was there. Maybe Mr. Jonas had been able to phone from the hospital to tell them he was coming. Nevertheless, Steve kept still. Nobody was going to say he didn't do his job to the letter, and that meant handing the package over to one man only, Mr. Brant.

"Well, I'll put on a little entertainment for you and be

back later." Arnie selected a record. "Here's something no red-blooded patriotic American kid can resist — the Military Marches of John Philip Sousa. Yah-dah-dee-dah-dah, dum-dum-dum-dum-dum-boom! . . ."

He left Steve with "The Stars and Stripes Forever" blaring in his ear, and Steve relaxed, glad to be alone. He reached for a lens paper, going automatically to his right hand pocket.

The pocket was wet.

Not sopping wet, but wet.

"Oh, gosh!"

What with his ankle and Arnie and Fred and all the other things that had been occupying his mind, he had not stopped to think about how wet his slacks had gotten.

What if a slosh of water had gone into his pocket? If those stamps got wet and stuck together, his name would be mud!

With frantic haste he dug out the package. He felt moisture on his hand before he had even looked at the wrappings.

They were soaked.

It was no time to hesitate. The vital thing was to get the wrappings off, dry the box, remove the stamps, and lay them out on something dry.

He tore at the wet wrappings and pulled out a small, flat, metal box. It glistened with tiny beads of water. He wiped it off on the front of his T-shirt. Then he opened the catch with his fingernail.

Steve had not known what fright was till then. Because what he saw in the small metal box was a folded, clear plastic envelope, and what shone through its transparency was not stamps.

In the envelope was a small gold coin Steve instantly recognized. It was an 1879 four-dollar gold Coiled Hair "Stella," one of the rarest of all U.S. coins. Only five were known to exist.

And one of those five had recently been stolen from the Belmont Collection.

10

PUT up for auction, the coin Steve was holding might have brought fifty thousand dollars. Remembering its picture, much enlarged, in the Belmont Collection catalogue, and the description under the picture, Steve recalled that the star on the reverse side had a faint scratch on its top point.

He peered closely at the coin in his hand, and his head swam. The scratch was there.

Shooting a terrified glance toward the door, he shut the box and jammed it and the wrappings back into his pocket.

Now he was in hideous danger, and he had trapped himself by unwrapping the package. If he handed it over now, Mr. Brant would know he knew what was inside.

When they found out he knew, what would they do with him? They could not let him go. But what would they do?

He was face to face with hard, cold, ugly reality. The empty television screen seemed to stare at him like a mocking reminder of all his comfortable daydreams. Here he sat in an armchair in front of the TV, but the action was on this side of the screen now, and there was no make-believe about it. He was feeling what the actors pretended to feel, but they were only acting, and they didn't know what it was really like to fear for your life. The most suspenseful crime show he had ever seen, safe at home in his own living room, had not prepared him for this.

What would they do? . . .

He had to get out of there, get away, find help somewhere. Forgetful of ice bag, ankle, and sprain, he stood up. But the moment he took his first step toward the door he was painfully reminded that he could not run away.

What would happen to him?

With a crash and a bang, "The Stars and Stripes Forever" came to a stirring conclusion. In the silence between it and the next selection he could hear the men talking outside, somewhere out in back.

"Hey, Fred, bring the wheelbarrow over here."

"Hold your horses, I'm coming!"

"Well, snap it up, I —"

Behind him the band launched into "The Washington Post" march, drowning out everything else. But by then Steve's first spasm of blind panic had passed, and he was thinking again.

He had thought of the telephone.

If only he could get to a telephone and dial the operator, he might be all right. He could tell her where he was and ask her to send the police.

If Arnie or Fred came in and found him phoning, he could say he was calling his mother. His one big advantage was that as yet they were not aware he knew anything he shouldn't. That being the case, there would be no reason for them to get excited about his calling home.

If only he could get a call through to the police, then all he would have to do would be to stall till they came.

Hopping along, bracing himself with his right hand

against the wall, he went up the hall and peeped through a doorway into what turned out to be a large living room.

He could have cheered and groaned all in the same breath. He saw a telephone, but at that moment it looked a mile away. It stood on a desk in a bay window on the far side of the room.

Gripping chairs and tables for support, Steve made a slow, tortured crossing of the room. Once he bumped his sprained ankle hard against a chair leg. The pain made him collapse into the chair with his head down, fighting nausea. A dozen deep breaths, and he was up again, with only a few more steps to go.

He cringed at the thought of standing exposed in that bay window, where anyone could see him, but he would have to do it. He was tempted to drag the phone down to the floor behind the desk, so as to stay out of sight. But what if they happened to come in and catch him at it? They would know right away he was up to something. No, he would have to stand there and act natural.

He was reaching for the telephone when a rumble outside warned him someone was coming. All thoughts of standing there in plain sight surrendered to instinct. He stumbled backward and ducked down behind the desk, grinding his teeth at the pain the effort cost him.

"Keep it straight, Fred, you're dribbling topsoil, and you know the King doesn't like to have good topsoil wasted."

That was Arnie, needling Fred, and the rumble must be coming from the wheelbarrow.

"Drop dead, will you?" snarled Fred. "I've had this gardening baloney up to here."

"That's what you think. Before you're through you'll

have it up to *here*. Can't you get it through your punchy head that this gives us a good image? The King knows what he's doing. Nothing is more respectable than raising flowers and planting shrubs. Not to mention buying antique furniture."

The King! Arnie must be talking about Kingsley Brant. And even if Steve had any doubts about the kind of men he was involved with, they were gone now. The way Arnie was talking, the things he was saying, took care of that. These men were crooks. Mr. Brant was a crook. Even old Mr. Jonas was mixed up with them!

The men had stopped in front of the bay window, apparently to work on a flower bed there. He could not make a call without their seeing him and hearing every word he said. If he stood up and went to the phone, they would want to know what he was doing. The thought of trying to act and speak naturally in such circumstances was more than he could handle. The hope that maybe they would soon move to another spot out of sight kept him where he was.

On pins and needles of frustration and impatience he listened to the rasp of a spade and the scrape of a rake as the men spread topsoil on the flower bed.

"Fred, you'd make a good gravedigger. I expect you've had some practice."

"Shut up about that, will you?"

"My, my, aren't we sensitive? Here, throw a little more of that stuff over here."

Time was passing, and each moment Steve was feeling more desperate, more trapped. He did his best to nerve himself to grab the phone and hope to reach the operator before they could run inside and stop him, but the thought of it made his spine turn into a column of ice. What if the operator didn't answer right away? Where would he be then?

What would they do to him?

The Arnie he heard talking to Fred was not the Arnie who had been nice to him a few minutes ago — and even then, some of his malice had leaked out from behind the mask. Steve had thought of several nasty things Arnie might be capable of doing to him when a new sound made his heart sink even further.

A car had turned into the driveway.

"Well, here's the King."

"About time!"

"Fred, you worry too much."

Mr. Brant was back! Steve came up to his knees, hands flat against the floor. Now what should he do? The car stopped. A car door opened and slammed. Footsteps tapped on asphalt.

"Did the boy show up yet?"

"He's here, King."

"Ah! Excellent!"

Mr. Brant's voice was high, silken, and cool. He seemed quite at ease, and well satisfied with the state of affairs. Arnie did not share his feelings. He had accused Fred of worrying too much, but now he revealed his own tensions.

"That old fool Jonas!" he snarled. "They were crazy to use him. He could have ruined the whole business. Of all the dim-witted things, sending a kid with —"

"Now, don't be too hard on Jonas." Mr. Brant's tone was that of a vastly superior person recognizing the limitations of his underlings. No wonder they called him the King. "Don't forget, Jonas thought he was dealing with nothing more than a few thousand dollars' worth of stamps in a perfectly legal transaction, and *that* was enough to stir up his ulcer. I'll admit it gave me a turn when I showed up at his office and found it closed. They told me across the hall he'd been taken to the hospital, but I didn't think it wise to try to visit him there. So I'm glad he had sense enough to phone here and let us know what he'd done, and I'm glad you had sense enough to call me at the upholsterer's. When did the boy turn up?"

Arnie described Steve's spectacular arrival, and the King chuckled while Steve blushed. Arnie made him sound like a clumsy idiot.

"I've got him stashed in my room with Fred's ice bag on his ankle and Sousa's marches on the record player, just to make sure he doesn't hear anything he shouldn't. I gave him a record to take home to his sister, and he's happy as a clam."

"Good. So he insisted he had to speak to me personally, did he?"

"That's right. I'll give him that much, he didn't tip his hand as to why he wanted to see you."

"Good. That speaks well for him. I'll give him a few dollars and then you can run him home."

"That's what I told him. I said I'd take him home as soon as you got back with the car."

"Splendid. Let's get this sofa out of the wagon and take it inside —"

"Aw, come on, now, King! Let's take care of —"

"Gently, gently! We don't want to seem to be in any frantic rush. Haste makes waste, gentlemen. Besides, I don't want the sofa to get any extra bouncing around when you take him home. I know how you drive. After all, that's why I picked it up myself. So lift it out carefully and carry it in, and then we'll go see young — what's his name again?"

"Steve."

"Young Steve."

A bare twenty feet from the men the trip-hammer under Steve's T-shirt was pounding so hard he half expected them to hear it. Despite the pain of dragging his sprained ankle along the floor, he did a high speed crawl partway across the room, then staggered to his feet and hobbled toward the doorway into the hall.

At first he was simply fleeing in terror, simply getting out of the living room before they came in carrying the sofa and found him there. He hopped down the hall to Arnie's room, not knowing what else to do, and turned into it.

His kite!

There it was, on the bed, and the sight of it brought back to his mind that preposterous idea he had dreamed up on the bus. It had made him laugh then, but now, suddenly, when he was desperate, it no longer seemed so laughable.

Like a drowning man grasping at a straw, Steve grabbed his kite case.

He spilled out the reel of string and the roll of stripping tape. Carrying them and his kite, he limped madly down the hall toward the back of the house. And down the hall behind him, sending his heart into his throat, came the sound of the front door opening. Though he was out of sight, Steve slowed down, being as quiet as he could.

The King's voice rose sharply.

"Hold it by the legs! Don't get your dirty hands on that upholstery!"

By the time the sofa came through the front door, Steve was easing himself out the back door.

11

STEVE held up his kite and prayed. Would the wind take it?

At ground level the breeze was unsteady and capricious. A gust caught at the kite and took it up a few feet while he swiftly paid out line, but then it sagged and almost dipped to the ground. A quick tug brought it up a few feet. It found a puff of air and climbed again.

"Steve? Hey, Steve!"

They had discovered he was missing, and Arnie was calling with a sharp edge of concern in his voice. Steve unreeled more line, concentrating with all his mind and will on getting the kite up into the steadier currents of the upper air.

When the back door was flung open, he might have laughed if he had not been so horribly frightened. A small, dapper man rushed outside, stopped short in surprise at seeing what Steve was doing, and was nearly bowled over by Arnie and Fred rushing out behind him.

"Watch it, you clods!"

Steve caught a flash of murderous temper in the small man's shrill outburst. But then he regained control of himself as swiftly as he had lost it. The face he turned toward Steve was smiling and benign, as though nothing could possibly have ruffled him.

From that moment on, Steve could not think of him as anything but the King. The air of a small, clever, cruel king sat on him like a mantle. If he had not known what he did, Steve would have been taken in completely. He would have accepted this pint-sized man with his thick-heeled, height-increasing shoes — he remembered the tapping sound on the asphalt of the driveway — as a kindly, cultured, rich stamp collector. He would have gone home with money in his pocket and a record for Amy, thinking how lucky he had been to bring him a set of valuable stamps from Mr. Jonas — Mr. Jonas, who might be a miser, but was not a crook after all!

The King even managed an indulgent chuckle that was like a pat on the head.

"Well! And what have we here!"

"I'm trying out my new kite."

"But I thought you sprained your ankle."

"I did, but I still figured I'd better fly my kite."

This strange statement made them bat their eyes. They glanced at each other, wondering if they had a junior lunatic on their hands. The King, however, was equal to the bizarre situation. He turned back to Steve with another smile as benign as the first one.

"Well, I don't blame you. It's a very handsome kite," he said, glancing up at it. Then he turned his gaze back on Steve, and though his smile remained in place, the eyes above it were bright and steely. "But I understand you wanted to see me."

"Maybe," said Steve. "I want to see Mr. Kingsley Brant."

"Splendid. That's me. What did you want to see me about?"

"I have a package for Mr. Kingsley Brant. Stay back!"

he warned sharply as the King took a step toward him. "I'm not taking any chances! Mr. Jonas said not to give it to anyone but him, and how do I know you're Mr. Brant? I don't even know this is really Ten Brookside Drive!"

The King had stopped, but now Arnie stepped forward.

"Listen, Steve, stop playing games —"

"Stay back or I'll let go!"

"Hold it, Arnie!" The King stopped him with a sharp gesture. "What are you talking about, Steve?"

Steve held up his reel of string.

"I'm not taking any chances! I taped the package to my kite, and until I'm sure you're really Mr. Brant I won't bring it down!"

The effect was impressive. Steve had never before seen three grown men turn pale all at once. Their eyes popped up at the kite, and popped at him. Arnie's face began to work, and his big hands clenched and unclenched as he measured the distance between them.

"Of all the stupid — Are you nuts?"

But the King held up his hand again.

"No. The lad is right. All he's asking for is proper identification, and he's perfectly right."

He did his best to recover his smiling composure as he clawed a wallet out of the inside breast pocket of his watermelon pink sports jacket and began pulling out cards. "Here you are. How about a credit card with my name on it and my picture on the back?"

Holding the reel away at arm's length with one hand, Steve stretched out his other hand for the card.

Edging forward as though approaching a bomb that must not be jarred, the King gave it to him.

Steve's close examination of the evidence was mostly pretense. His glasses were so fogged up he could scarcely see it. But he handed it back with a nod.

"Okay. I'm sorry, Mr. Brant, but Mr. Jonas told me to be extra careful."

"Well, you can certainly tell him you were," said the King in a double-edged tone of voice. "Now, what say you bring your kite down and deliver that package? And for heaven's sake be careful. As I'm sure you know, we're dealing with some valuable stamps there. I wouldn't want anything to happen to them."

"No, sir. I'll reel it in."

Steve began slowly taking up string. The kite was high now, and under good control. After a moment he stopped to free one hand, take off his glasses, and wipe them awkwardly across his shirt front. It seemed to him he could almost hear teeth being gnashed impatiently around him. But he needed to see better, because this next maneuver was going to be the trickiest of all. It was doubly hard, too, because it went against the grain. He hated to do it, but there were times when sacrifices had to be made.

The wind could not have been in a better quarter for his purpose. He was able to bring the kite down squarely over the big shade tree in the corner of the yard.

"Hey, watch out!"

It was Arnie who yelled as, all at once, the box kite swooped sideways and down. Steve closed his eyes tight for the instant of impact. He could not stand watching his brand new handmade kite crash into tree limbs and branches.

The deed was done. The kite was hung up in the tree. Arnie yelled something unprintable.

"Oh, gosh! I'm sorry!" cried Steve. "The wind caught it and — Golly, if my ankle was okay I'd climb up and get it, but — Have you got a ladder?"

The King's face was pale again, and this time his smiling composure had sideslipped like the kite and was just as thoroughly demolished. He held his rage on a leash, but the leash was taut.

"I hope nothing has happened to that package," he said with a white-lipped expression that made Steve hope he would never be at this man's mercy.

"Oh, it'll be okay. I put it on with a whole lot of stripping tape!"

The King stared at him briefly, a terrible, quiet stare, then turned and said, "Fred, get the ladder."

Both Fred and Arnie hurried toward the garage. The King started walking toward the tree.

"I'm going to get the ice bag," moaned Steve, "my ankle is killing me!"

The King glanced back at him as though he would have enjoyed helping the ankle do the job, and said, "Go ahead."

Sweating and suffering, Steve dragged himself to the back door as fast as his good leg would carry him.

Now to get to the telephone!

He had just made it to the bay window when for the second time that day he saw a welcome sight. This time it was shattering. It made him forget all about telephoning.

Officer Joyce's cruiser pulled into the drive and stopped beside the King's station wagon.

The sight was too much for Steve. What little strength

he had left went out of him. He gripped the corner of the desk, then dropped into the chair behind it as the room threatened to go black. He put his head down, and the terrible giddiness passed. But then relief surged through him and he thought he was going to cry. Maybe a few tears did get away from him. At any rate, his eyes blurred. He could hardly see a thing. Taking off his glasses, he dragged the edge of a short sleeve angrily across his eyes, gave his glasses a quick wipe, and put them on again.

By that time Officer Joyce was out of his car and the King was walking toward him. Over by the tree Arnie was holding the ladder. Fred had climbed it and grunted his way up onto a thick branch. He was reaching up for the kite. They both turned to look at the policeman, their faces expressionless.

The King produced an easy smile as he ambled forward.

"Good afternoon, officer. Can I help you?"

"I hope so. Where's Steve O'Neill?"

"Steve? Why, he's inside, putting an ice bag on his ankle. Poor lad sprained it falling in the brook on his way here."

"I figured that must be his kite I saw. What's he doing over here?"

"Oh, it's quite all right, officer, he wasn't trespassing. Actually, he came looking for me, because he had a package for me. And now, would you believe it, my package is up in that tree."

The King was good, no doubt about that. He made the whole thing sound like a whimsical joke. By that time Steve had mastered himself enough to feel he could appear in public, so he left the King explaining how the package happened to be up there, and hobbled to the front door.

When he opened it, another car was in the driveway. A taxicab.

Out jumped Fox Face.

Steve staggered forward in a panic.

"Watch out, Officer Joyce! Here comes another one!"

The officer spun around, startled. He saw a surprised man in dark glasses who had stopped to stare at Steve, and he saw Steve pointing at the man.

"He's a crook! He followed me!"

Fox Face looked amazed.

"Relax, Steve," said Officer Joyce. "He's a detective."

"Hi, Steve. My name's Finelli. What have you been up to, anyway? Here, let me help you. Looks like you've had a little accident."

And so it was that Steve found himself being helped along by — of all people — Fox Face.

"Mr. Brant tells me you brought him something, Steve," began Officer Joyce.

The King cut in smoothly.

"That's right, officer, he did. It's a set of postage stamps from the Jonas Coin and Stamp Company. Very valuable, too, worth several thousand dollars."

He turned and looked toward the tree, toward the kite, and his voice had a carrying quality as he added, "I certainly hope that kite brought them down safely. I'd hate to lose them."

Steve understood what the King was doing. He felt sure Arnie and Fred got the message, too.

The package was to be lost. No package, no evidence.

No embarrassing possibility of having to open it up in front of a police officer and a detective.

By then Fred had pulled the kite down to him.

"Hey!" he cried. "Where did he put it? There ain't no package stuck to this kite! It must have fell off!"

Fred spoke with a conviction that would have been hard not to believe.

Steve, for one, believed him.

"That's all right," he said, more to Detective Finelli than anyone else. "I didn't have time to stick it on the kite, I only said I did. It's still here in my pocket."

He produced the little box and handed it to the detective.

"It's not stamps, either. It's a coin."

Detective Finelli opened the box and looked. The four-dollar "Stella" gleamed golden in the sunshine.

12

WELL, at least he had been right about one thing: the reason Mr. Finelli had followed him.

"We were pretty sure the ones who pulled the job in New York had given the coin to Jonas for someone here," the detective explained, "and we were pretty sure he would take it to his office and turn it over to someone who came to see him there —"

"Did you think Mr. Jonas was one of the crooks?"

"Yes, I'm afraid we did. So we followed him. But then his ulcers kicked up and he called the rescue squad before we even had a chance to stake out his office."

He had the whole family for an audience, because by that time it was several hours later and Steve's father had come home early from his office.

"So naturally, when we went upstairs and there was this wild-eyed boy in the hall who told us where Jonas was and then left as fast as he could, I smelled a rat. Any kid who didn't hang around at a time like that had something on his mind. At least, that was my hunch, and I followed up on it."

"But why did they send the coin to Brant?" asked Mr. O'Neill.

"The sooner the thieves got the loot out of New York

and spread around, the better, as far as they were concerned. Big-time thieves are always afraid of informers, and they don't want to be caught with the goods in their possession. But already, within the last couple of hours, several arrests have been made in three or four cities, and I expect most of the Belmont Collection will be recovered."

"This Brant fellow — what about him?"

"I think we'll find he was an important fence who did a lot of traveling, probably abroad, where there are plenty of collectors who aren't fussy about where their prize items come from."

"How did you know to come to his house when Steve was there?"

"Well, when Steve jumped into the woods, I was in a taxi coming his way. I hopped out and talked to Joyce. When he said Steve had mentioned an errand he had to do, I filled Joyce in on what I thought Steve was involved in.

"He drove around the woods in one direction and I went the other, hoping to catch Steve coming out. We kept checking the boulevard, too, in case he crossed. Finally Joyce came tearing along in his cruiser. 'I saw his kite up,' he said, and took off, and as soon as the cab could get turned around I followed him."

"And neither of you thought of the culvert," said Steve, pleased with that part.

"No, although as things turned out it was just as well, because as it was we really nailed them," said Mr. Finelli, and laughed. "I'll never forget that scene. Brant standing there turned to stone, the blond guy jerking around so fast he knocked the ladder down, and that big ape swinging by one arm in the tree yelling for help. It was beautiful."

Steve laughed, too, but a bit absently. There were so many angles to consider that his mind had gone on to another question.

"I wonder what Mr. Jonas will think when he hears what happened?"

"He'll get another ulcer," said his father. "This business put him in the hospital, and now he won't see a dime out of it."

"And I won't see a Cent out of it," said Steve, managing a sorrowful little joke.

"Listen, he ought to be grateful to you," said Mr. Finelli. "You're the one who can testify he was an innocent go-between who thought he was delivering stamps."

"You don't know Mr. Jonas," sighed Steve.

Later on, when he was alone in his room reading, he took stock of the situation.

Across the hall the Lowest Common Denominators were polluting the atmosphere with their latest hits. Arnie was right. This collection was their worst. When Mr. Finelli had helped him return to Arnie's room to collect his kite case, Steve had mentioned the record. Mr. Finelli unhesitatingly handed down a judgment.

"Okay, he gave it to you, he said he didn't want it any more, and where he's going he won't need it. So you take it!"

And what had it got him? A lot of squeals and a bear-hug. If there was anything worse than a scornful sister, it was a grateful sister.

Besides that, in the way of things to show for his outing, he had a sprained ankle and a smashed-up kite. And no Fugio Cent.

Oh, well. Someday . . .

But you never know.

On his birthday a small package arrived by special messenger. And in it was the Fugio Cent.

What's more, Mr. Jonas never even asked Steve for the ten dollars.